Illustrated by Guell

A Random House PICTUREBACK® Book

Random House 🏠 New York

Copyright © 1993, 2001, 2009 Disney Enterprises, Inc. All rights reserved. Published in the United States by Random House Children's Books, a division of Random House, Inc., 1745 Broadway, New York, NY 10019, and in Canada by Random House of Canada Limited, Toronto, in conjunction with Disney Enterprises, Inc. Previous editions of this work were published by Western Publishing Company, Inc., in 1993 and by Random House Children's Books, a division of Random House, Inc., New York, in 2001. Pictureback, Random House, and the Random House colophon are registered trademarks of Random House, Inc.

Library of Congress Control Number: 2001089604

ISBN: 978-0-7364-1317-6

www.randomhouse.com/kids

Printed in the United States of America

18 17 16 15 14 13 12 11 10 9

Second Random House Edition

*O*nce upon a time, there lived a beautiful young princess named Snow White. Her hair was as dark as night, her lips were as red as a rose, and her skin was as white as snow. Snow White was so lovely that her stepmother, the Queen, was very jealous of her. So the Queen dressed Snow White in rags and forced her to clean and scrub the castle.

Each day, the Queen asked her magic mirror, "Magic mirror on the wall, who is the fairest one of all?"

And each day the mirror replied, "You are the fairest one of all."

One day, while Snow White was working in the courtyard,
a handsome Prince suddenly appeared. Snow White was
so shy that she ran back into the castle. The Prince sang to
her through an open window. As she listened, Snow White
realized that this was the Prince of her dreams!

That afternoon the Queen asked, "Magic mirror on the wall, who is the fairest one of all?"

But this time the mirror replied, "Snow White."

In a rage, the Queen summoned the Royal Huntsman. "Take Snow White into the forest and kill her," she commanded.

The Huntsman led Snow White deep into the forest. But Snow White was so sweet and lovely that he could not bring himself to harm her.

"Run away!" the Huntsman told her. "Hide and never come back."

Snow White raced through the dark woods. Her heart
was pounding with fear. A cold wind nipped at her heels.
Snow White's dress got caught on a twisted tree branch,
and she tripped on a thick root and tumbled to the ground.

Snow White lay there, sobbing. When she dried her
tears and looked up, a group of friendly animals stood all
around her. The gentle creatures listened to Snow White's
sad story, then quickly led her through the woods.

Snow White followed her new friends to a charming little cottage. "It's just like a doll's house!" Snow White exclaimed. "I like it here." And since the door was open, she walked right in.

Inside the cozy cottage were a long wooden table and seven tiny chairs. "There must be seven children living here," said Snow White. "Seven *untidy* children," she added, looking at the dust and cobwebs all around her.

Suddenly, Snow White had an idea.

"If we clean the place up," she told her animal friends, "perhaps they'll let me stay!"

And so they all went to work—washing and wiping and cleaning the clutter.

When the room was clean as could be, Snow White went off to explore the rest of the cottage.

Upstairs, Snow White found a big room with seven little beds. Each bed had a name carved on it: Doc, Happy, Sneezy, Dopey, Grumpy, Bashful, and Sleepy.

"What funny names for children," Snow White thought. "Speaking of Sleepy, I'm very tired myself." So she lay down across three of the beds and quickly fell asleep.

That night, the owners of the cottage returned. But they
weren't seven little children—they were the Seven Dwarfs!
And when they saw their clean and tidy house, the
Dwarfs immediately knew something strange was going on.

All Seven Dwarfs crept upstairs and found Snow White stretching and yawning under the sheets. They thought she was a monster!

"Let's attack it while it's sleepin'," Doc said.

But just then Snow White popped her head out and said, "How do you do?"

By the time Snow White had finished her sad story, all the Dwarfs wanted her to stay with them—except for Grumpy.

"We'll protect you from the Queen," they told Snow White.

At the castle, the evil Queen had learned from her magic mirror that Snow White was still alive. So she decided to get rid of the girl once and for all.

Calling upon her evil powers, the Queen made a potion that would transform her into an ugly old hag.

Then, using her book of magic, the evil Queen created a poison apple.

"One taste and Snow White's eyes will close forever!" she cackled.

There was only one cure for the Queen's sleeping spell—love's first kiss.

That same night, Snow White and the Seven Dwarfs sang and danced into the wee hours.

Before they went to sleep, Snow White told the Dwarfs a bedtime story—all about the handsome Prince of her dreams.

Early the next morning, Snow White made the Dwarfs apple pancakes. Then she gave each Dwarf a kiss on the forehead as he left to work in the diamond mines.

"Beware of strangers," the Dwarfs warned. Then they marched off, cheerfully singing, "Heigh-ho, heigh-ho! It's off to work we go!"

As Snow White began her chores, an ugly old woman suddenly appeared.

She held a big red apple out to Snow White. "They're delicious, dearie," she said.

Snow White's animal friends didn't like the old woman one bit. But kindly Snow White invited her inside anyway.

"This is a magic wishing apple," the old woman said. "One bite and all your dreams will come true."

Snow White, who knew a lot about dreams but little of evil, reached for the apple and took a bite. And her animal friends, who knew this was not a harmless old woman, raced off to find the Seven Dwarfs.

The Dwarfs arrived at the cottage just as the old hag was leaving. They chased her through the woods and up a rocky cliff. Higher and higher she climbed, with the Dwarfs close behind. When she reached the top, a storm suddenly brewed. Lightning crashed down, sending the hag shrieking over the edge.

The Seven Dwarfs found Snow White in a deep, deep sleep. They felt so sad that they made the beautiful princess a bed out of solid gold and vowed to watch over her forever.

It wasn't long before the Prince, who had been searching far and wide for the fair Snow White, rode up to the cottage.

The Prince knelt beside the sleeping Snow White. Then he leaned down and kissed her. Snow White's eyes fluttered open. She was alive!

The Seven Dwarfs danced with joy.

Then the Prince lifted Snow White onto his white horse and they rode off together—to live happily ever after, of course.